Modern Curriculum Press
BEGINNING TO READ Series

MODERN CURRICULUM PRESS

The Shy Little Turtle

Phylliss Adams
Jean Strop

Illustrated by: Mary Ann Dorr / Creative Studios I, Inc.

Softcover edition published simultaneously in Canada by
Globe/Modern Curriculum Press, Toronto.

Library of Congress Cataloging in Publication Data

Adams, Phylliss.
  The shy little turtle.

  Summary: Sandy, a turtle, is too shy to start a friendship until
she discovers some good ways to make friends.
  [1. Turtles — Fiction.   2. Bashfulness — Fiction.
3. Friendship — Fiction.   4. Stories in rhyme]   I. Strop, Jean,
1950-   .   II. Dorr, Mary Ann, ill.   III. Title.
PZ8.3.A216Sh   1985   [E]   85-13719

ISBN 0-8136-5171-9 **(hardbound)**
ISBN 0-8136-5671-0 **(paperback)**

1 2 3 4 5 6 7 8 9 10   87 86 85

There lived a small mud turtle,
In a field with a pond near by.
She often felt quite lonely,
Because she was so shy.

Sandy would sit all by herself,
And watch the other turtles play.
She wanted them to ask her to join,
But when they did, she would crawl away.

She would crawl until she found a place
Where she was hidden well.
Or if she couldn't find one,
She would hide inside her shell.

One day while she was hiding,
She decided the thing to do
Was to learn how to make friends,
So she wouldn't be lonely and blue.

She soon came up with a plan,
And let out a loud "Yahoo."
She'd watch all the other turtles,
To find out what they do.

The next day she climbed on a rock.
In her shell she partly hid.
She watched each kind of turtle
To see the things they did.

First Sandy watched the painted turtle,
For she wasn't hard to see.
Others liked her pretty colors,
Colors bright as they could be.

The painted turtle didn't say much
When others would come near.
But she let them see her pretty shell
Instead of crawling away in fear.

Next Sandy watched the great big turtle,
Who was very tall and wide.
He let others climb on to his back,
And gave them all a ride.

Sandy saw that the little ones
Feared the big turtle for a while.
But he got them to come near him
With a nod and a friendly smile.

Then Sandy watched the snapper,
The turtle who could bite.
But the others weren't afraid of him,
Since he did not ever fight.

Instead he gave them bugs he caught,
And chased mean turtles away.
He made the pond a safer place
For all his friends to play.

Next Sandy saw a turtle
Who was shaped just like a box.
She moved so slowly through the field,
She looked just like the rocks.

This turtle did not seem special.
In fact, she seemed quite plain.
But she had more friends than anyone —
A hard thing to explain.

So Sandy watched her closely,
To see what she would do.
She'd walk up to a turtle and say,
"I'd like to be friends with you."

Sandy sat and thought about
The things other turtles had done.
She decided she would try
To do those things, one by one.

The very next day Sandy began
Talking to a turtle that she knew.
They talked about the things they liked
To watch, and hear, and do.

To Sandy's surprise, that turtle
Talked for a long long while,
Then stayed and played all day with her,
And Sandy crawled home with a smile!

The next day Sandy thought
Of a different thing to try.
She would practice being friendly
By smiling and saying, "Hi."

She said "Hi" to everyone
She met near the pond that day.
They smiled, and said "Hi" right back,
In a very friendly way.

Though Sandy had some friends now,
She kept trying just the same.
She would ask someone to play with her,
And share her favorite game.

She was still feeling a little shy,
When she saw a new turtle by the tree.
But she went up to him and said,
"Please come and play with me."

This new turtle pulled into his shell,
And Sandy knew he was shy too.
So she stayed right there and said again,
"I'd like to be friends with you."

The new turtle peeked out at her,
And slowly began to smile.
So Sandy started talking to him,
Smiling all the while.

Now Sandy has a lot of friends,
They talk and laugh and play.
Although she is still a little shy,
She makes new friends each day.

If you feel shy but want some friends
There are things that you can try.
You can ask them, you can share a game,
Or you can smile and just say, "Hi."

Modern Curriculum Press

BEGINNING
TO
READ
Series

ISBN 0-8136-5671-0